OLIVIA™
Trains Her Cat

D0595294

adapted by Sarah Albee, based on the screenplay
"Olivia and Her Trained Cat" written by Joe Purdy
illustrated by Shane L. Johnson

Ready-to-Read

Simon Spotlight
New York   London   Toronto   Sydney

Based on the TV series *OLIVIA*™ as seen on Nickelodeon™

SIMON SPOTLIGHT
An imprint of Simon & Schuster Children's Publishing Division
1230 Avenue of the Americas, New York, New York 10020
For information about special discounts for bulk purchases, please contact Simon & Schuster
Special Sales at 1-866-506-1949 or business@simonandschuster.com.
Manufactured in the United States of America 0213 LAK
20 19 18 17 16 15 14 13 12
Library of Congress Cataloging-in-Publication Data
Albee, Sarah.
Olivia Trains Her Cat / adapted by Sarah Albee ; illustrated by Shane L. Johnson. — 1st ed.
p. cm. — (Ready-to-read)
"Based on the TV series, Olivia as seen on Nickelodeon"—Copyright page.
I. Johnson, Shane L, ill. II. Olivia (Television program) III. Title.
PZ7.A317401 2009
[E]—dc22
2009011862
ISBN 978-1-4424-1383-2 (hc)
ISBN 978-1-4169-8296-8 (pbk)

"My cat, Gwendolyn, can jump," says Francine.

"Wow!" all of the kids say.

"And Gwendolyn can also walk on her back legs," says Francine.

"My cat, Edwin, can dance ballet!" says Olivia.

"Wow!" all of the kids say.

"Gwendolyn can cook,"
says Francine.
"So can Edwin!"
says Olivia.

"Your cats sound special," says Mrs. Hoggenmuller. "Can you bring your cats for show-and-tell?"

"We can have a pet talent contest!" says Olivia.

"Great idea!" says Mrs. Hoggenmuller.

"Edwin just likes to sleep,"
says Julian.
"Will Edwin do tricks?"
Olivia is sure that
Edwin will.

"Okay, Edwin, jump!"
commands Olivia.
Edwin keeps sleeping.

"If you jump through
this hoop, you can
have a fish!"
Edwin just snores.

"Is something wrong, Olivia?"
asks Mother.

"Edwin will not do tricks!"
says Olivia sadly.

"He just sleeps!"

"It is hard to get an old cat to do tricks," says Mother.

"But Francine has a cat that will do tricks!" groans Olivia.

The next day at school,
the talent show begins.
"My hamster can eat
a carrot," says Daisy.
Everyone claps.

"My parrot can say 'hi,'"
says Harold.
"Hi, there!" says the parrot.
Everyone claps.

"This is my lizard,"
says Julian.

"He can catch a fly."

Everyone claps.

"This is my cat, Edwin," says Olivia.

"Edwin can do many tricks."

"Jump, Edwin!" says Olivia.
Edwin sleeps.

Oh, no! Olivia worries.

"Okay, then, sleep, Edwin!"

Edwin sleeps.

"Snore, Edwin!"

Edwin snores.

Everyone claps.

Francine goes next.
"Meet Gwendolyn."

She can walk on

her back legs.

She can flip backward.

She can jump
through a hoop.

"I think we have a winner!
The winner is Gwendolyn!"
says Mrs. Hoggenmuller.

After school Olivia
and Julian go to her house.
"Edwin should have won,"
says Julian.

Olivia looks around.

"Where is Edwin?"

Olivia and Julian

search and search.

Olivia and Julian go
to Francine's house.
They find Gwendolyn.
They also find Edwin
doing tricks!